Understanding GENDER IDENTITY

Don Nardo

San Diego, CA

For more information, contact:
ReferencePoint Press, Inc.
PO Box 27779
San Diego, CA 92198
www.ReferencePointPress.com

LIBRARY OF CONGRESS CATALOGING-IN-PUBLICATION DATA

Names: Nardo, Don, 1947- author.
Title: Understanding gender identity / by Don Nardo.
Description: San Diego, CA : ReferencePoint Press, Inc., 2022 | Includes
    bibliographical references and index.
Identifiers: LCCN 2021018780 (print) | LCCN 2021018781 (ebook) | ISBN
    9781678201784 (library binding) | ISBN 9781678201791 (ebook)
Subjects: LCSH: Gender identity--Juvenile literature. | Gender
    nonconformity--Juvenile literature.
Classification: LCC HQ18.552 .N37 2022 (print) | LCC HQ18.552 (ebook) |
    DDC 305.3--dc23
LC record available at https://lccn.loc.gov/2021018780
LC ebook record available at https://lccn.loc.gov/2021018781

Contents

Man into Woman

"I am like a wretched grub which is waiting to become a butterfly."[1] These words were spoken in the 1920s by Danish artist Einar Wegener. Born in 1882, he was about to become the first known person to undergo surgery involving a change of gender. The personal road he had trod to reach that moment had been long and in some ways torturous. In 1902, at age twenty, he had married fellow artist Gerda Gottlieb, and in the years that followed the two remained close and reasonably happy.

Nevertheless, as time went on Wegener felt increasingly uncomfortable in his male body. He began to feel as though he shared that body with a second personality, a female whom he came to call Lili. "I was obsessed by the delusion that this body did not belong to me alone," he later wrote in his diary. In a way, he went on, "my share in this body grew less day by day, as it enclosed in its interior a being which demanded its existence at the price of my existence. I seemed to myself like a deceiver, like a usurper who reigned over a body which had ceased to be his, like a person who owned merely the façade of his house."[2]

Wegener reached a turning point of sorts when, one day in 1908, his wife was awaiting the visit of an actress friend. Gottlieb had planned to draw her friend wearing various outfits. At the last minute, however, the actress was unable to make it, so Gottlieb persuaded her husband to pose in those outfits for her instead. As Wegener donned women's clothes, he underwent an unexpected and surprisingly strong emotional reaction. He later recalled:

> When all was ready we could scarcely believe our eyes. I turned round and stared myself in a mirror again and again, trying to recognize myself. Was it really possible, I asked myself, that I could be so good-looking? . . . I cannot deny, strange as it may sound, that I enjoyed myself in this disguise. I liked the feel of soft women's clothing [and] I felt very much at home in them from the first moment.[3]

A Totally Unprecedented Operation

Thereafter, the inner personality whom Wegener called Lili Elbe became more and more prominent in the young man's life. With the blessings of his wife, who made it clear she was primarily interested in his personal stability and happiness, Wegener cross-dressed frequently in the apartment. Sometimes close family friends were present, and on the whole they were supportive and nonjudgmental.

As Lili Elbe grew increasingly important to Wegener, he concluded that he must be an extremely rare individual whose body housed twin beings, one male and one female. At the same time, he began undergoing serious discomforts, including major nosebleeds. Trying to make sense of what was happening to him, he read numerous books on human sexuality. But neither those sources nor the several doctors he consulted had any clue what was causing his symptoms.

Eventually, the confused artist decided that there was only one path for him. He must find one or more doctors who would agree to do something extraordinary—namely, perform surgery that would transform him into a woman. After finding a physician who was willing to perform what was then a totally unprecedented operation, the patient wrote in his diary, "The operation is urgent, and the doctor would like me to proceed to Berlin immediately, as some twenty days must elapse between the first examination and the operation."[4]

The surgery gave Wegener the outward physical characteristics of a woman, and he began calling himself Lili Elbe on a regular basis. But over time he felt that these changes were too superficial. He actually longed to become a woman *internally* as well, hopefully in such a way that would allow him to have a baby. Such a transformation is beyond even today's advanced medicine, so in the early twentieth century it was, in doctors' minds, pure fantasy. Yet Lili Elbe insisted. And in 1931 she managed to find a doctor who would attempt to implant a uterus in her body. Sadly, the operation failed. Elbe developed a severe infection and died at age forty-nine.

Educating the Public

A biography of Lili Elbe, which incorporated large sections of her diary, appeared in 1933 and has never gone out of print. This is

Actor Eddie Redmayne is seen here in his Oscar-nominated role as transgender artist Lili Elbe in the well-reviewed 2015 film The Danish Girl.

in part because over time other people, from nations around the globe, came forward to say that they too harbored mixed feelings of the male and female genders within them. Eventually, the term *transgender* was coined to describe such a condition.

Later still, in 2015 a major film based on Elbe's life, *The Danish Girl*, made headlines and won numerous awards. It stars Eddie Redmayne, who received an Oscar nomination for his portrayal of Elbe. That film was instrumental in introducing millions of people to the idea that alternate gender identities besides the traditional male and female exist. Redmayne himself acknowledged what he saw as a crucial social obligation to capture both the facts and emotions involved in Lili Elbe's unusual life. "I'm being given this extraordinary experience of being able to play this woman," he told an interviewer. "But with that comes this responsibility of not only educating myself but hopefully using that to educate an audience."[5]

> "I'm being given this extraordinary experience of being able to play this woman."[5]
>
> —Eddie Redmayne, Academy Award–winning actor

Chapter One

Many Alternative Gender Identities

Jessy was born in Thailand. But his parents moved to the United States when he was an infant, and he grew up in Cooper City, Florida. Now in his twenties, he says that the first time he can remember his gender being an issue in his life was when he was three. "I had a lot of boy friends," he recalls, "and we were always playing with toy guns. One day I went into the boys' bathroom with them, and my mom pulled me out. 'You can't go into that bathroom.' I was heartbroken." Then the child asked, "Why can't I go into that bathroom?" The mother answered, "You're a girl. You have to act like one. You can't always be with the boys." From that moment on, Jessy says, "I knew that being a girl is not me. That is not how I feel."[6]

As the years went on, Jessy continued to feel like a boy and did "boy things" whenever possible. Those included taking karate and boxing lessons. Because he was still bio-logically a female, he also joined the girls' basketball and soccer teams at school.

In the tenth grade, seeing so many classmates dating, Jessy wanted to do the same. But he did not want to date boys, because he was attracted to girls. At that point, he started to suspect that he might be a lesbian, or a girl who is attracted to other girls. But it soon became clear that the sit-uation was more complicated than that. "The thing was," he remembers, "although I dated lesbians, I was attracted to straight women. I was attracted to girls who like men."[7]

As still more time passed, Jessy realized that he was not a lesbian, after all. It became clear to him that he was attracted to straight girls because, despite his female appearance, in his mind's eye he was a straight male. He realized that he must be transgender. He eventually underwent a physical gender transition that included hormone treatments and became what he had long realized he was—a man.

Now a young adult, Jessy says that he cannot erase the fact that he was born in a girl's body. That is a fact of his life, he states. But he is grateful that he went through the transition. "God made me transgender for a reason," he asserts.

> "God made me transgender for a reason."[8]
>
> —Jessy, transgender man in his twenties

> Maybe not God, but whoever created me. Whoever created me made me this way for a reason. I enjoy life from a different perspective. I can see the world simultaneously from a male and female perspective. When I speak with [my girlfriend], I understand where she's coming from as a woman. . . . And then, when I speak to my male friends, I get along with all the guys 'cause I think like a guy. I always thought like a guy.[8]

Age-Old Assumptions About Gender

One major reason that Jessy went through so many years of confusion in trying to understand his true gender is that society as a whole has not yet fully shed some age-old misconceptions about gender. A majority of people not only in the United States but in most parts of the world see themselves as either male or female. Moreover, there has long been and remains a general assumption that those are the only possible genders that human beings can be.

Some transgender boys will pursue activities they perceive as masculine, such as karate.

It remains unclear whether one's gender identity—each person's internal experience and feeling of gender—starts right from birth. Scientists are in general agreement, however, that most people have an awareness of their gender identity by about age three. At that age, children do not have the intellectual ability to understand this, but they can feel it in an intuitive, or instinctive, sense.

Gender identity is about, or is rooted in, who a person is in his or her brain or mind's eye. Alana Biggers, a professor at the Chicago College of Medicine, explains:

Gender identity is your own personal understanding of your gender and how you want the world to see you. For many cisgender [strictly male or female] people, gender identity is automatically respected. When most people encounter a normative [regular] cisgender man, they treat him as a man. This means acknowledging his autonomy and using the correct pronouns—he/him/his—when addressing him. It's important to treat everyone with this level of respect.[9]

Only Two Possible Genders?

Throughout most of human history, the vast majority of people assumed that gender was binary in nature; that is, that there were only two possible genders: male and female. A newborn baby was seen as either a girl or a boy. In the traditional binary system, therefore, if a person was born with female genitals, or sex organs, she was a girl; likewise, if a newborn baby had male genitals, he was a boy. A great many of the ideas, customs, and traditions of most cultures are based on this seemingly simple binary determination of physical characteristics, says Trent University psychologist Karen L. Blair. Among numerous others, these ideas, customs, and traditions include

> "Gender identity is your own personal understanding of your gender."[9]
>
> —Alana Biggers, Chicago College of Medicine professor

the clothing we buy, barbershops vs. salons, and men's rooms vs. women's rooms. In fact, one of the first things new parents often learn about their future child is their sex, based on a grainy ultrasound image of tiny little genitals. From this point forward, a parent's idea of who their child will grow up to be is significantly shaped by the sex, represented through the color of the nursery room, the types of clothing purchased, and of course, the list of potential baby names. Our expectations based on gender do not stop there. When we find out that a baby is a boy, we are more likely to describe him as strong, tough or handsome, whereas we will view baby girls as sweet, gentle and kind.[10]

Although most people fit within this binary system of gender, many individuals do not. These individuals have recognized that although they were born with the physical form of a male or female, they do not perceive themselves as that gender. They may instead view themselves as a man trapped in a woman's body

Gender Identity Versus Sexual Orientation

Gender identity and sexual orientation are two different things. Gender identity is the gender a person identifies with. Sexual orientation is who, or which gender, a person is attracted to. For example, a person who identifies as female sees herself as a woman. Depending on her sexual orientation, she might be attracted to men or she might be attracted to other women.

This can be confusing, even to some trans and nonbinary individuals. For instance, Christina, a young trans-woman, explains her initial confusion, saying that early on, "I *thought* I was gay because I was attracted to men. But I'm attracted to straight men, not gay men. Before I educated myself about what being transgender really is, I thought that I must be a gay person." Then Christina read an online medical article that explained the difference between gender identity and sexual orientation. It also noted that a trans person can be either straight or gay. Thus, a trans woman like herself, who was born with a male body and is attracted to men, is straight, not gay.

Quoted in Susan Kuklin, *Beyond Magenta: Transgender Teens Speak Out*. Somerville, MA: Candlewick, 2014, p. 43.

or a woman trapped in a man's body. These people are today referred to as transgender, or "trans" for short.

Transgender individuals have long felt the need to hide their true selves, but this is changing. In recent years a number of trans individuals, including some well-known celebrities, have come out, or publicly revealed their gender identities. In 2020, for example, actor Elliot Page, who turned thirty-three that year, did so. During the bulk of his career, including when he received critical acclaim and an Oscar nomination for the 2007 film *Juno*, he had been actress Ellen Page. Even when making that movie, he says, he felt as if he was a young man trapped in a young woman's body. He adds that this feeling caused him shame and discomfort. But over time, he says, "I was finally able to embrace being transgender and let myself fully become who I am." He underwent a physical transition from female to male and says he is happy "now that I'm fully who I am in this body."[11]

A Diverse Spectrum of Identities

From a technical standpoint, Page and other trans people *do* fit into a binary system, since they identify as either male or female. However, it is not the *traditional* binary system, in which an individual always retains the gender identity with which he or she was born. As a result, transgenderism is an alternative binary gender system.

Similarly, some individuals feel they belong to still another alternative gender system. They do not see themselves as fully male or fully female. Instead, they describe their gender identity lying somewhere between, or perhaps beyond, the traditional two gender variants.

Actor Elliot Page, formerly Ellen Page, attends a film premier in 2019. Page, who came out as transgender in 2020, is one of many public figures to recently do so.

Today mental health professionals and others say that these people belong to what is often referred to as the "gender spectrum." It is best described as a collection of many different individual gender identities that do not conform to a two-gender system. Because they appear to exist outside the binary concept of gender, they are generally referred to as nonbinary.

The gender spectrum is extremely diverse, and nonbinary folk can and do express a range of gender identities so wide that it can seem confusing. The popular online health care website WebMD tries to simplify the concept somewhat with this brief thumbnail sketch:

> Non-binary is also spelled nonbinary, and sometimes shortened to "NB" or "enby." Non-binary people often identify as gender-nonconforming, as well. There are many individual identities that are grouped under the term non-binary. Some include:
>
> • a-gender, or a person without any specific gender identity;
> • bi-gender, or someone who identifies with two or more genders;
> • genderfluid, or a person whose gender identity frequently changes;
> • genderqueer, or someone with a specific gender that is not a binary gender.[12]

Ancient Cultures

Whether they identify as trans or nonbinary, people expressing alternative gender identities are not a recent psychological or social phenomenon. Indeed, evidence suggests that they have always existed in human societies. Archaeologists discovered the oldest example to date of such evidence in 2011 in the Czech Republic when they unearthed a grave site almost five thousand years old.

Views on Gender Conformity

In the following passage, Trent University psychologist Karen L. Blair explains how nonconforming gender behavior is generally viewed within the traditional, widely accepted binary gender system.

The extent to which men conform to stereotypical masculine behaviors and interests and the extent to which women conform to stereotypical feminine behaviors and interests can be described as gender conformity. When individuals stray from their expected gender roles—or behave in gender nonconforming ways—they tend to be evaluated negatively, although such negative views are not meted out equally. For example, men who possess feminine qualities or interests are often evaluated much more harshly than women who possess masculine interests or qualities. One does not need to look any further than the differing connotations applied to the concepts of a tomboy girl versus a sissy boy to see how society responds differently to gender nonconformity as a function of whether one is adopting or abandoning masculinity.

Karen L. Blair, "Has Gender Always Been Binary?," *Inclusive Insight* (blog), *Psychology Today*, September 16, 2018. www.psychologytoday.com.

The site yielded a number of burial artifacts, including the well-preserved skeleton of a human male.

What immediately struck archaeologist Kateřina Semrádová and the other excavators was the skeleton's odd positioning. As the Archaeology News Network explains:

Whereas male skeletons from that culture are usually found buried on their right side with their heads facing the East, this [body] . . . is interred on its left side with the head facing the West, the traditional position for female burials. An oval, egg-shaped container usually associated with female burials was also found at the feet of the skeleton. None of the telltale objects that usually accompany male burials, such as weapons . . . were found in the grave.[13]

Semrádová told interviewers that she and her colleagues were convinced they had found one of the earliest examples of a third (or alternative) gender burial. She also reported that archaeologists had on occasion found very ancient graves in which women were interred in ways usually associated with male burials.

In some later ancient cultures in Europe, the Middle East, and southern Asia, religions emerged that seem to have attracted alternatively gendered people, perhaps because the leaders of those faiths accepted such individuals. Male priests of those religions often presented themselves as having either female traits or no specific gender traits at all. Many were eunuchs—men whose genitals had been removed. Historians doubt that all of these priests were trans or nonbinary, because some likely were castrated simply out of religious custom.

A Long Legacy

Moreover, the gods of some of these ancient cultures displayed various characteristics that today are associated with trans and nonbinary people. One such deity, Hermaphroditus, worshipped in what is now Turkey, had a mixture of female and male traits. Similarly, in Greek mythology the blind prophet Tiresias was sometimes a man and other times a woman. His ability to take on both genders at will was widely viewed as a blessing bestowed by the gods.

In real life, meanwhile, the Roman emperor Elagabalus, who came to power in 218 CE, appears to have had an alternative gender. It is unclear whether he was trans or nonbinary, but evidence shows that he regularly wore female attire and makeup. According to the second-century-CE Roman historian Dio Cassius, the young ruler "sometimes wore a hair-net, and painted his eyes, daubing them with white lead and alkanet [a dye made from an herb]." Elagabalus also plucked out all the hairs in his chin "so as to look more like a woman." Documented as well was that he wanted to literally become a woman physically. Dio recorded that "he asked the physicians to contrive a woman's vagina in his body by means of an incision, promising them large sums

16

for doing so."[14] (Evidently the emperor never went through with such surgery, for if he had done so, his ancient biographers would surely have mentioned it, whether he survived or not.)

Historians have found similar evidence for alternatively gendered people in late ancient, medieval, and early modern times. One such individual who especially stood out was German writer Karl Heinrich Ulrichs (born in 1825). As a child he consistently told his parents that he was really female at heart and wanted to become that way physically. In his adult years he boldly fought for women's equality in a society still almost totally controlled by men. Long after his death, in the late twentieth century, his writings were rediscovered, and he became a hero of the emerging modern trans community.

In 2021, the US Senate confirmed Dr. Rachel Levine (pictured) as assistant secretary for health in the US Department of Health and Human Services. She is the first openly transgender official to achieve a major federal government position.

In later years other individuals, like Ulrichs, became well known for blazing the way for trans and nonbinary folk to be recognized and eventually accepted in society. Prominent among them was the first known trans person to undergo a surgical transition from male to female—Einar Wegener, later called Lili Elbe. Arguably more famous was the first American to undergo gender-transition surgery, Christine Jorgensen (born in 1926). She had the operation quietly in 1951, but less than a year later some American newspaper reporters revealed her secret, igniting a controversy. Although uncomfortable with the mostly negative notoriety she received, she managed to endure it and thereafter devoted herself to educating the public about trans issues.

Gender Identity No Longer an Issue?

As more decades passed, increasing numbers of Americans became aware that alternative gender identities existed. Moreover, it became clear to many that a person with such an identity can be no less productive a member of society than someone with a traditional binary gender. As a result, eventually a few trans and nonbinary individuals began to make it into high-profile public positions.

An important milestone in that respect was the US Senate's confirmation early in 2021 of Pennsylvania native Dr. Rachel Levine as assistant secretary for health in the US Department of Health and Human Services. The first openly trans official to achieve a major federal government position, Levine was previously a professor at the Penn State College of Medicine and Pennsylvania's secretary of health. "With very few exceptions my being transgender is not an issue,"[15] Levine told a reporter. Indeed, she pointed out, every person, regardless of gender identity, should be judged "strictly on [his or her] professional qualifications."[16]

> "With very few exceptions my being transgender is not an issue."[15]
>
> —Dr. Rachel Levine, US assistant secretary for health

Chapter Two

Being Transgender

Now in his twenties, Illinois native Hayden Reid did not start to suspect he was transgender until he was nineteen. He had long known that although he had been born in a girl's body, he secretly wanted to be a boy. He recalls, "When I was a kid I often went to bed praying to God to let me wake up and be a boy. What I hadn't realized until recently was that I have always been that boy. I just didn't match physically to what I was born as mentally."[17]

Eventually, from reading books and articles and seeing stories about transgender people on television, Reid realized that he was not unique and not mentally warped in some way. Instead, he had an alternative gender identity. After mulling things over for a while, he decided it was time to share his secret with others. At age twenty, he says, "I came out to my step mom and my dad as transgender and started to see a therapist about it."[18] Soon after that he came out to his closest friends. He also got a haircut that made him look more masculine and began wearing men's shirts. In addition, he replaced his female first name with Hayden, which he felt was a suitable male name.

When a major newspaper asked him to summarize how he felt about being trans, Hayden wrote, in part:

I feel more confident in my skin than I have ever before. I never thought something like this was possible, but now I have realized that it is okay to be

myself. When I first started realizing that I was transgender
. . . I blocked it away. I never thought it was an option for
me. . . . Now that I have started my journey as Hayden
Reid I have realized that I can be him, that I *am* him. Looking in the mirror, I see the young boy more and more. He's
maturing and becoming stronger.[19]

When Body and Brain Do Not Match

In reading about the basics of transgenderism, Reid learned that
what makes a person trans is an inconsistency, or imbalance,
between that individual's biological gender and gender identity.
Biological gender is normally based on the genitals a child has at
birth. In contrast, gender identity reflects brain chemistry, which in
a sense "tells" the child it is male or female. In the vast majority of
cases, biological gender and gender identity conform, or match
each other. So a child born with a male body also possesses
strong emotional feelings that consistently confirm to him that he
is a boy. Likewise, most children born with female physical characteristics feel mentally and emotionally that they are girls.

Now and then, however, the two principal gender-related
factors—biological gender and gender identity—do not conform. The result is a baby born transgender, with a body and
a brain chemistry that contradict each other. This nonconformity, or gender mismatch, is the root of the most prevalent self-
description voiced by trans people—that one is either a male
trapped in a female body or a female trapped in a male body.

Jessy, for example, who was born Jessica and spent his
young childhood in Cooper City, Florida, often felt like there was
a boy lurking within his female body. That did not seem right to
him, and he frequently worried that he might be mentally ill. "At
first," he later recalled, "I thought maybe there is something psy-
chologically wrong with me because I was feeling this way. Am I
abnormal? I was a little insecure. I didn't have anyone to talk to. I
had to work through it on my own."[20]

Transgender people exist in every country in the world. This young trans woman is seen taking part in an LGBTQ pride parade in Guwaheti, India.

Similarly, Kimberly felt that she was a woman trapped in a man's body. Bearing a male body and name, as a child and adolescent she did all the things a healthy young boy was expected to do, including playing sports and dating girls. Her male manifestation joined the US Marines, fought in the Iraq War, got married, and became a father. "Yet all the while," she remembers, she knew there was something wrong on a basic level, perhaps something seriously abnormal. "I struggled with something fundamental inside me," she explains.

> I fought being transgender tooth and nail. I thought that I could replace this feeling I could not articulate with self-discipline and self-control. I buried it down deep into a little compartment until, like leaking acid, it started to burn a hole through my soul. One day I realized that despite my best efforts "it" was still there and I was 35 years older. Obviously, whatever "it" was, was not going to go away. At that time I decided to quit fighting and to accept that I am transgender.[21]

A Confused Youth Turns to YouTube

Nikki Hayden, an English trans woman in her twenties, here recalls how she figured out that she was transgender.

> Until I was about four or five I didn't know I wasn't a girl, to be honest with you. One of my earliest memories, about five years old, was being yelled at by a teacher for going to the toilet with the girls. . . . School was extremely difficult. I got bullied a lot. I was picked on for being too thin, for being feminine, for not liking football, for hanging round with girls, for having long hair. They mocked everything they could think of in terms of gender and sexuality. I learned what trans meant through YouTube. I knew how I felt but I didn't know there was a term for it. I was basically just trying to Google what I felt. A lightbulb went off in my head and I thought, this explains all the issues I've had as long as I can remember.

Quoted in Kate Lyons, "Transgender Stories: 'People Think We Wake Up and Decide to Be Trans,'" *Guardian*, 2016. www.theguardian.com.

As Normal As Being Left-Handed?

In one form or another, Jessy, Kimberly, and Hayden Reid all experienced that fear of being abnormal, of being some sort of rare aberration or freak. In fact, such worries are quite common among trans people when they are young and struggling to understand who they really are. However, extensive scientific research has shown that they are not abnormal after all.

Instead, trans folk, along with nonbinary and gay people, constitute so-called normal deviations in society. A common documented example of a normal deviation is left-handedness. Although most people are right-handed, scientists say it is normal for a certain minority of the members of each new generation to be left-handed. Before the early twentieth century, it was widely presumed, even by some scientists, that the minority status of "lefties" made them somehow abnormal and thereby inferior to "righties." In some parts of the world, therefore, parents and teachers forcefully made lefties write with their right hand in an effort to make them "normal."

Another familiar minority condition in the human spectrum that used to be viewed as abnormal is having blue eyes, since a majority of people have brown eyes. Scientists now know that it is normal for a minority of people in each new generation to have blue eyes. Similarly, it is typical for a minority of people to be left-handed; normal for a small percentage of the population to be gay, natural for a small proportion to be nonbinary, and normal for a small percentage to be trans.

As for exactly how many Americans are transgender, no one knows for sure. But a number of experts working for a variety of reputable organizations have made general estimates based on polls and surveys. Among others, these include the US Census Bureau in 2015, the California-based research group the Williams Institute in 2016, and the respected LGBTQ advocacy group GLAAD in 2017.

Transgender people, along with nonbinary and gay people, constitute so-called "normal deviations" in society, much like being left-handed in a world full of right-handed people.

In 2020 the well-known polling organization Gallup completed a major study on this topic. The study combined information from prior surveys with completely new interviews with more than fifteen thousand American adults age eighteen and older. Gallup estimated that at least 2 million US adults are transgender. The organization cautioned that this number is likely somewhat low because some people tend to be reluctant to reveal such personal information about themselves. "To the extent [the survey] reflects older Americans not wanting to acknowledge an LGBTQ orientation," Gallup senior editor Jeffrey M. Jones states, the "estimates may underestimate the actual population prevalence of it."[22]

Deciding Whether and When to Come Out

Another reason that the Gallup estimate of the number of trans adults is likely too low is that it does not take into account trans individuals who have not come out yet. In the LGBTQ community, to come out is to admit to family and friends, and perhaps others, that one is gay, bi, trans, or nonbinary. At any given moment in time, some trans people either do not yet know they are transgender or do not feel ready to let others know. So they have not yet come out.

> "For young people who feel distressed about their gender, puberty can be a very difficult and stressful time."[23]
>
> —National Health Service

The coming-out process can occur at a wide variety of ages. Some people realize they are transgender when still in their preteen or early teen years and decide to come out then, at least to parents, close friends, or both. For those very young people, reaching puberty is most often (though not always) the moment of awareness about their gender identity. According to Great Britain's National Health Service, "For young people who feel distressed about their gender, puberty can be a very difficult and stressful time. This is the stage where your assigned gender at birth is physically marked by body changes, such as the growth of breasts or facial hair."[23]

A Female-to-Male Transition

Mark was born biologically female and until his teen years bore the name Marcy. Eventually, he realized he was transgender, and over time he transitioned, a process he describes here.

Transitioning for me meant finding the path out of a deep, dark closet of repression and denial. That took 26 years and some tremendously dedicated therapists. I remember something I told that first counselor when I was just about ready to let the light in: "It's like I'm standing on a precipice looking into a chasm, about to take a leap of faith." Once I opened that door, my feet were set on the path to becoming a physically recognizable male. After practicing cross dressing in public, I began weekly testosterone shots, which lowered my voice, changed the shape of my face and body, and made me sprout facial peach fuzz. As a testament to my motivation to cross that gender role bridge, I legally changed my name three days after I had my breasts surgically removed. That took place about six months after I left the closet. Within five years, I had additional surgery to remove female reproductive organs and have some male reconstruction.

Mark, personal interview with the author, April 8, 2021.

Jessy experienced this negative reaction to such changes in his female body. "Breasts!" he recalls. "I was starting to develop breasts. Oh crap. I hated bras, never liked wearing them."[24] For Jessy, reaching puberty was a wakeup call informing him that he must seriously consider coming out.

Other trans individuals wait till they are in their mid- to late teens to come out, as was the case with Declan Nolan, a trans man from Wayland, Massachusetts. He announced that he was a boy, not a girl, in his freshman year of high school.

> "I was starting to develop breasts. Oh crap. I hated bras."[24]
>
> —Jessy, Florida trans man

Moreover, he did so in an unusually creative manner—by making a film. Through making and showing it, he remembers:

> I started to tell my friends and family about my gender identity. As those I loved accepted me, I grew to accept myself. In May 2013, [my film] "Ross" premiered at my high school's film festival in front of hundreds of students, faculty, and families. It was overwhelmingly positively received. I didn't get one negative comment that night. Since then, I've posted the film online and . . . I get numerous comments and emails from viewers telling me how they can relate to the character and that they've used the film to explain gender identity to their families and friends.[25]

In contrast, Cass Averill of Eugene, Oregon, was in his twenties when he realized he was a trans man. A computer security specialist at a major tech firm, he came out to his manager and recalls that "his response blew my mind."[26] Averill's boss was hugely supportive, as were family members and friends who learned the news.

Not all trans people are fortunate enough to receive such positive reactions to their coming out. Some encounter rejection. For example, the National Center for Transgender Equality says that about 10 percent of trans people who come out to their families report being physically harmed by a relative. And roughly 8 percent of those who come out as trans are kicked out of their home.

However, experts point out that this situation is steadily changing for the better. Acceptance of transgender individuals is growing. Personal acquaintance could be one factor. A Kaiser Family Foundation (KFF) poll published in June 2020 found that 36 percent of adults know someone who is transgender. This might also explain the large percentage of people (68 percent) who say they support laws that ban discrimination against transgender individuals.

Initially, trans man Cass Averill (pictured), worried about negative reactions to his coming out. However, his coworkers strongly supported him.

To Transition or Not?

A few trans folk do not come out until they are middle-aged or elderly, and an undetermined percentage *never* end up coming out. The same broad range of ages and personal decisions surround another important aspect of the transgender experience — transitioning, or adjusting one's life in order to be the gender one identifies with. Two general ways to accomplish such a transformation exist. In the first, the person does not resort to surgery or other major physical interventions. Rather, he or she usually undergoes a name change to better match the newly assumed gender.

The individual may or may not also cross-dress, or wear the clothes most often associated with the identified gender. This is not done to achieve sexual satisfaction, educator and social worker Nicholas M. Teich points out. Not all cross-dressers are trans or otherwise LGBTQ, but when trans people cross-dress, Teich says it is "because it makes them feel more genuine."[27]

Other trans people decide that changing their name and wearing gender-appropriate clothing do not go far enough. Often they opt instead for a more comprehensive approach, which can include hormone treatments, gender-affirmation surgery, or both. For some, the hormones alone prove more or less satisfactory. In a male-to-female transition, the subject receives the female hormone estrogen, which will steadily make breasts grow and may also broaden the hips. Conversely, in the case of a female-to-male transition, the chief hormone involved is testosterone. It will make the subject grow more body hair, gain some muscle mass, and in some instances have a deeper voice.

Statistics indicate that 25 to 30 percent of trans people in the United States undergo surgery in addition to taking hormones. In general, the surgery alters the person's genitalia to reflect the true gender identity. Those who choose this procedure first go through a preparatory period in which they live as the gender they identify with. Thus, a biological female who seeks to transition into a male must initially live as a man for a while—usually a year or more. Most often this approach prevents a surgical candidate from proceeding too fast and having the operation without thoroughly thinking it through.

In most cases, during that transitional period the person also prepares family, friends, and coworkers for the upcoming change. Depending on the individual circumstances, this process can be stressful. It can also be smooth and uplifting, as it was for Averill. He gratefully remembers that after he revealed his gender identity to his boss at the tech firm, the two

> developed a plan for navigating my transition that considered all parties affected. It started with a mass email, where I came out to over 300 colleagues in one fell swoop. The second the email was sent it was as though all the air in the building had been sucked out. . . . Within moments I had people approaching my desk to shake my hand, give a hug or offer encouraging words. Not once did I hear a peep of negativity. Not once![28]

To Achieve Comfort and Happiness

Although only a minority of trans folk go through a transition that includes surgery, those who do are almost always satisfied with the results. According to New York–based plastic surgeon Millicent Odunze, "Quality of life appears to improve after gender-affirming surgery for all trans people who medically transition. One 2017 study found that surgical satisfaction ranged from 94% to 100%."[29]

Whether or not trans individuals choose to transition, they—like other people—seek some measure of comfort and happiness. And much of that depends on how one is treated by others. In the words of Loren Bornstein, a trans man from Portland, Oregon, "A person shouldn't have to prove who they are to you by their personal, private body for you to respect them for who they are." He adds, "We don't have to understand people to love and accept them, but it does help. All we are asking is for a little respect."[30]

> "We don't have to understand people to love and accept them."[30]
>
> —Loren Bornstein, Portland, Oregon, trans man

Chapter Three

Being Nonbinary

"How can I explain myself to someone normal?" asks Nat, a native of New York City who is now in his twenties. "[It's] hard to explain. Usually I don't like to use labels, but if I did, I would say I'm gender queer, gender neutral, or simply queer." Nat uses the term *queer* in the manner adopted by LGBTQ folk in recent times, not in the derogatory way it was used in past eras. "It means I'm neither male nor female," he goes on. "I'm a whole different gender, a third gender, so to speak."[31]

About his background, Nat explains that his birth certificate indicated he was female. Moreover, he *looked* like a girl, in that he had female genitalia. He says:

> I thought you follow whatever's on your birth certificate. But maybe that isn't always true. Everyone always said I was weird, so that's how I considered myself. That's 'cause I was called a freak in middle school. And weird. A weird freak! I was taller and broader than most girls. I looked like a girl—but not exactly like a girl. I acted like a boy, but I wasn't a boy. When people became more sexual, around eighth grade, everyone assumed I was gay or lesbian."[32]

Nat says that he was not gay, but he could sense a difference between himself and other students. In those days, he was not yet familiar with the term *nonbinary*. So when asked to describe himself, he would simply say, "I consider myself both male and female." That is, he felt as if he had elements of both genders imbedded within him. "I had an image in my head," he continues, of being "androgynous, in between, as if you can't tell that I have male or female genitalia."[33]

With such images floating around in his head, it is perhaps not surprising that Nat "felt weird because I still couldn't express myself." Worried about his mental well-being, he searched for answers in books about human sexuality and looked at many photos in books and online. "I learned that there are people who look like both sexes but are not both sexes," he says. "They're another gender—a third gender. You know how during the Renaissance the portraits seem androgynous? I was attracted to that."[34]

A Term Often Hard to Define

Today Nat feels more comfortable about his gender identity because he knows he is not alone but rather part of a community that exists in nearly every town and city in the world. Although possibly not as numerous as gay and trans people, nonbinary folk are far from rare. Experts estimate that there are at least six hundred thousand nonbinary individuals in the United States alone, and the actual number could be significantly higher. (The reason is that millions of people identify as bisexual. Evidence suggests that some of them are confusing their sexual orientation with their gender identity, and those who are doing that may actually be nonbinary.)

One problem in trying to ascertain the size of the nonbinary community is that the term itself is not universally recognized. Furthermore, even those who do know the term do not always agree on what it means. "As more people use the word nonbinary to describe themselves," officials at GLAAD explain, "it has become its own umbrella term. Non-binary now means many different things to different people."[35]

For this reason, it is sometimes difficult for nonbinary people to describe how it feels to be nonbinary. In the words of Kylan

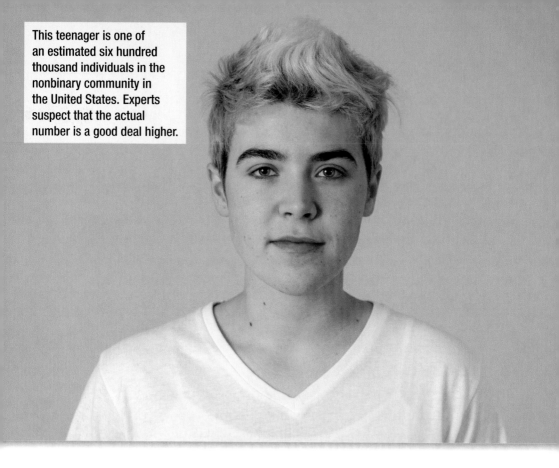

This teenager is one of an estimated six hundred thousand individuals in the nonbinary community in the United States. Experts suspect that the actual number is a good deal higher.

Camburn, a nonbinary GLAAD representative who does online social commentary, it is indeed often hard to precisely define being nonbinary.

> The non-binary community is diverse and each experience is different and nuanced. When asked about my own gender, I often repeat something I've heard said by gender nonconforming and non-binary people: I am me-gender. I am simply myself, despite any parts I may have been born with. Who we are is often affected by how society views us, but how we identify is entirely about how we view ourselves. To exist outside strict definitions is powerful and also vulnerable, which is why I admire non-binary people who are able to live their lives honestly. Living openly as non-binary is a statement made to society that says we can be more than what we were told to be.[36]

The Spectrum's Tremendous Diversity

The personal outlook of another nonbinary individual strongly reinforces Camburn's description of people living "their lives honestly." In an interview with Camburn, New Yorker Danni Inman states:

> Being non-binary means that I can always be my most authentic self. That it doesn't matter whether I'm a man or a woman, because I'm neither. I was never meant to fit into the mold, because the mold doesn't fit me. Being non-binary means to me that I can be my masculine self and my feminine self all the time because both of those parts of me make the whole. I never felt more like myself, my true, whole self, then when I came out as non-binary. Being non-binary means I get to be free.[37]

Many other nonbinary people describe the same feeling of freedom of personal expression that Inman does. However, that does not answer the question of where on the human gender spectrum they feel they belong. Almost all nonbinary folk say they feel neither fully male nor fully female. Instead, they claim to fall somewhere in the middle, or maybe even beyond, the spectrum's traditional male-female extremes. Figuring out one's place within that wide range can be confusing at first, especially for a young person who is still struggling with the concept of personal gender identity. Nat, for instance, recalls his own gender-related confusion when in the eighth grade: "I started to notice that my body was changing. But I wasn't developing like girls. When I tried to compare myself to boys, I wasn't like them either. So where the hell should I go? . . . I don't want to sound like a victim, or whatever, but I constantly asked myself, 'What am I?'"[38]

Nat's efforts to find the proper place in the gender spectrum, along with the same struggle that thousands of other nonbinary

> "I constantly asked myself, 'What am I?'"[38]
>
> —Nat, who identifies as nonbinary

folk endure, demonstrates that spectrum's tremendous diversity. It is a fact confirmed by the large, at times daunting number of terms that nonbinary people use to describe themselves. One of the most common is *genderqueer*, sometimes expressed simply as *queer*. Some nonbinary individuals use those words in a general sense, as umbrella terms synonymous with *nonbinary*. But others see genderqueer or queer as a subdivision of nonbinary, lying somewhere between traditional male and female gender identifications. Exactly where in that range a person falls can vary markedly from one individual to another. One person who identifies as queer in that sense states:

> I started identifying as genderqueer about two years ago. My now-wife was the catalyst. Neither of us had ever really identified with the 'lesbian' label, and we started to question what else was out there. For a while, I wondered whether I might be trans, because I knew I wasn't fully female, but [after realizing I was not trans] I started looking into what 'queer' actually meant. That opened a whole world of labels, sub-labels, and categories, and genderqueer was the one that fit.[39]

From Bi-gender to Gender Fluid

In addition to *genderqueer* and *queer*, nonbinary people employ numerous other terms to describe their gender-related feelings. One, *bi-gender*, is most often used in a general sense and, like *queer*, tends to denote that a person possesses elements of both male and female. In contrast, some members of the community identify as *a-gender*, which is also sometimes expressed as *gender neutral*. These terms essentially mean that the person feels no particular affinity for any gender. Instead, that individual feels unique, as if belonging to a third or fourth gender.

A nonbinary person who uses the name Dakota, who is now almost thirty, says that strong feelings of having no set gender ini-

The Feeling of Not Being Alone

Almost all nonbinary people have their own personal views about who they are gender-wise, and with rare exceptions no two members of the nonbinary community describe their feelings in the same manner. The following perspective is by a self-described nonbinary young woman named Athena Schwartz, a research assistant at the Utah Department of Human Services.

> What being non-binary means to me is staying true to myself. Non-binary has no look and no one can tell you if you are non-binary or trans "enough." . . . You don't have to be out to everyone and you don't have to be out at all. You are non-binary because that is how you identify. No one knows you better than you. You're in charge of your identity. It also means community to me. I am so grateful for all of the chosen family members that I have met just from coming out and reaching out. I have learned so much from the other non-binary people I have met through this journey. I have learned that I will never be alone. There will always be someone who has had a similar experience or a similar feeling. It just might take a little time finding.

Quoted in Kylan Camburn, "9 Young People Explain What Being Non-Binary Means to Them," GLAAD, July 14, 2019. www.glaad.org.

tially surfaced at age nineteen: "I began to figure out my a-gender identity. I'm a sort of subset of genderqueer. [I] feel like I don't really have a gender at all. I don't feel male or female. I have elements of both sexes, or maybe neither."[40]

Twenty-eight-year-old James also identifies as a-gender and makes the point that there is no strict definition for it:

> There are a lot of different ways to feel and be a-gender. Like any identity category, people who identify as a-gender have different ideas of what that means. . . . An a-gender person may present solely femininity or masculinity, or may move between the two, or may blend them to create a sort of nonbinary style. . . . Or the lack of gender may mean that they don't think about [gender] at all. Everyone is different, obviously.[41]

The smiling people seen here reflect the tremendous diversity of age, race, and gender that exists in the broad alternative gender spectrum.

Still another nonbinary category consists of individuals who feel that their gender is not fixed or static but rather changes over time. Most of those who feel that way call themselves gender fluid, or simply fluid, although some use terms such as *pangender* or *polygender*. Twenty-five-year-old Cam, from Ireland, claims to have had the inner feelings of multiple genders. At one point, he recalls, "I came across another word: fluid flux. This fits with me because I experience several genders but they vary in intensity. They are socially constructed genders inasmuch as I would probably have described them differently in another civilization, but the feeling is still innate."[42]

Cam's use of the phrase "socially constructed genders" is crucial to the discussion of nonbinary feelings of gender. By that, he means that from time to time various people in society may and do invent new descriptive terms to fit how they see and feel about themselves. And that may well be true when it comes to words describing genders.

Indeed, a number of experts point out, nonbinary subdivisions such as queer, bi-gender, a-gender, and gender fluid are, from a strictly scientific standpoint, not necessarily separate genders equal in weight to male and female. Rather, most of these terms are better understood as labels used by people who do not fit into traditional societal gender modes in order to find clarity, express themselves, and feel good about themselves. As Janani, an Indian behavior analyst, says, "There are no rules with how people use identity labels; you put five genderqueer people in a room and they will all likely define 'genderqueerness' differently, but what they'll probably have in common is how the label helps them feel and move in the world."[43]

Centuries Worth of Precedents

Nevertheless, some experts think that members of the nonbinary community may represent a separate or third gender. There are solid precedents to support that view. As Meghan Werft and Erica Sánchez of the prestigious international organization Global Citizen point out, "Cultures in regions from Oaxaca State, Mexico to Samoa and Madagascar have accepted the idea of the 'third gender' for centuries." On the island of Madagascar, they note, the Sakalava people have long

> recognized a third gender called Sekrata. Boys in Sakalava communities who exhibit traditionally feminine behavior or personalities are raised by parents as girls from a young age. Instead of labeling these boys as gay, they are seen as having a male body and identifying as a female. Sexual preference is not a factor for the Sakalava and raising a child in this third gender is natural and accepted in the community's social fabric.[44]

37

A similar cultural tradition evolved in the southern sector of Mexico's Oaxaca region. There live the locally respected and accepted muxes, defined as biological boys who identify as neither male nor female. Over the centuries, they became known for their skills as cooks, craftworkers, and nannies. One muxe, who goes by the single name Felina, states, "We're a third [gender]. There's men and women and there's something between, and that's who I am."[45]

Fernando Noé Díaz, a local schoolteacher who has several muxe friends, explains how the muxes have become woven into society's social fabric: "When the man is at sea or in the field and the woman is at the market, there is no-one to take care of the household and family. That's where the muxe comes in. Some even say it's a blessing for a mother to have a muxe son who will help her at home and take care of young siblings."[46] Muxes have long been important members of local Catholic church congre-

Among Mexico's large community of muxes is Grecia Jiménez Osorio, seen here, who ran for mayor of her town, Tlactepec, in 2018. Muxes, defined as biological boys who identify as neither male nor female, are respected and accepted. Over the centuries, they have become known for their skills as cooks, craftworkers, and nannies.

Equal Parts of Male and Female?

One common nonbinary category is androgyny. Androgynous people feel that they lie roughly halfway between male and female on the gender spectrum, as explained by one of their number, Lane Patriquin:

> I am an androgyne. I have been androgynous my whole life, but it was very difficult for me to accept my own identity once I discovered it. There was so little information available. It was extremely lonely knowing deeply that this was what I was, but having no access to information about how or why I was this way or what to do about it. It was very difficult for me to have my identity respected, or to justify it to anyone in my life in a way they could understand. I tried for a very long time to make myself keep living as a female, and when I couldn't do that any longer I started living as male. But when it came down to it, this was the only thing I could be and still be healthy and happy. Both masculinity and femininity are equal parts of who I am, and I cannot be just one or the other without denying an essential part of my identity.

Quoted in *New York Times*, "Lane Silas Patriquin," 2015. www.nytimes.com.

gations as well. Churches in the region have accepted the tradition of three genders for centuries.

Several cultures in the Pacific islands, along with some in southern Asia, have very similar third-gender traditions, as do at least 155 separate Native American tribes. Evidence for their existence in those societies dates back centuries. Among the Native Americans, each tribe had its own name for trans and nonbinary people. The Lakota called them Wiakte; the Navajo called them Nadlesh; to the Crow they were the Batee; to the Zuni, the Ihamana; and to the Ojibwe, the Lkwekaazo.

Today all of these names fall under an umbrella term coined in the twentieth century—*Two-Spirit* people. It is meant to describe two separate spirits—one male, the other female—inhabiting a single body. Many Two-Spirit Native Americans wore women's clothes. Most of them performed traditional female tasks, including food gathering, cooking, mediating in local disputes, and fulfilling various spiritual duties for the community. No less importantly, nearly all were accepted members of their respective tribes.

Models of Enlightened Attitudes

Some experts suggest that the existence and decent treatment of the Two-Spirit folk, along with similar examples of third-gender traditions from around the globe, is instructive. That is, such examples have value as possible models for less enlightened and less accepting modern societies. The experiences of the Sekrata, muxes, Two-Spirit people, and others like them show that it is possible to be both inclusive and tolerant of nonbinary people in any society. In the words of a twenty-one-year-old American nonbinary individual who uses the name Khalypso,

> Society must understand we're regular people and we do everything people with binary genders do. Stop being afraid of us and stop . . . misgendering us [insisting we must be either male or female] and take the time to learn more about the history of gender. . . . We're human beings and we really do just want to live like everyone else.[47]

Chapter Four

Social Challenges of the Alternatively Gendered

In 2018, having reached his eighteenth birthday, Oliver, a resident of the Washington, DC, area, was looking forward to voting for the first time. When he entered his polling place to cast his ballot in the midterm election, he showed his ID to one of the volunteer workers. After a few seconds the worker appeared confused and said that there seemed to be a problem. The ID card stated its owner was female and, clearly, Oliver was male.

At that point, Oliver politely explained that he is transgender and was, at the time, undergoing a transition. He had already legally changed his name, but he had not yet updated his ID to exhibit his new gender identity. It came down to money, he said, because it was "a really expensive process."[48]

The poll worker asked Oliver to wait while she spoke with a supervisor. After some discussion, Oliver was allowed to vote. This experience left him feeling frustrated. It is an example of one of the many daily challenges encountered by transgender and other alternatively gendered individuals. Some of these challenges stem from bias. There have been many instances in which trans or nonbinary people experienced discrimination in housing or job interviews or were refused medical care, insulted, threatened, harassed, beaten, and in some cases even killed. An example of the latter occurred in February 2021 in Ambridge, Pennsylvania. Sixteen-year-old trans boy Jeffrey "JJ" Bright and his sibling Jasmine Cannady, a twenty-two-year-old nonbinary person, were shot to death by their mother. As of April, police and prosecutors had not publicly stated a motive for the killings.

Those tragic fatalities were "at least the eighth and ninth violent deaths of transgender or non-binary people in 2021," reports Madeleine Roberts of the Human Rights Campaign. "We say 'at least' because too often these deaths go unreported. . . . As this high rate of violence against [alternatively gendered] people continues, we need everyone to keep mobilizing, keep speaking up, and keep supporting trans and non-binary lives."[49]

The Problem of Entrenched Transphobia

For some of those who mourned Bright and Cannady, the key question was *why* someone would kill them. Experts say that the immediate reasons for hatred, discrimination, and violence vary from case to case. But overall, a major element inherent in these incidents is the inability to understand or accept the differences that characterize individual people. According to the California-based research and advocacy group Gender Spectrum, "As one of the most fundamental aspects of a person's identity, gender deeply influences every part of one's life. Where this crucial aspect of self is narrowly defined and rigidly enforced, individuals who exist outside of its norms face innumerable challenges. Even those who vary only slightly from norms can become targets of disapproval, discrimination, and even violence."[50]

> "Those who vary only slightly from norms can become targets of disapproval, discrimination, and even violence."[50]
>
> —Gender Spectrum, California-based advocacy group

Such negative reactions to alternatively gendered folk, experts say, tend to be triggered by various degrees of transphobia. This is hatred or fear of trans and nonbinary people. Like

42

Young people place flowers at a memorial set up in Ambridge, Pennsylvania, to honor slain trans man Jeffrey "JJ" Bright and his nonbinary sibling, Jasmine Cannady, who were murdered by their mother.

homophobia, hatred or fear of gay people, transphobia is not nearly as widespread and intense today as it was in the past. In the early post–World War II era, for example, it was particularly entrenched in American society. In the words of documentary film maker Bennett Singer, "There was a new push toward conformity after the war, a return to normal political life and social life. Embedded in that was this sense of heterosexuality—that men should marry women and that women should have kids and be subservient. This fitted the classic model of what a healthy society was."[51]

In the decades that followed, however, intensive research by scientists in a variety of fields showed that the underpinnings of homophobic and transphobic thought are based on unfounded and cruel stereotypes. This has been confirmed by numerous studies by members of the American Medical Association,

No Help from School Staff

The recollection of Utah high school student Kevin of having adult school staff blame him for the bullying he suffered and refuse to help him is not an isolated case. A Massachusetts college student named Larry, who describes himself as a member of the LGBTQ community, spent many of his school years in Kansas. He recalls seeing a group of football players bully another LGBTQ youth in a school corridor while a teacher watched and did nothing. "Bigger guys were always sucker-punching him when he was looking the other way," Larry remembers,

> and he seemed to nearly always have a black eye. That time I saw the football jocks jump him, they threw him against the wall so hard he fell on the floor. They kicked him while he was down and one of the social studies teachers saw it all and didn't do a damn thing to help him. He actually laughed right along with the jocks and they all just left him there laying on the floor, holding his stomach, where they'd kicked him. I felt so bad for him, but I was also super-glad it wasn't me.

Larry, personal interview with the author, November 20, 2019.

American Psychiatric Association, and dozens of other leading medical and health care organizations.

The problem, leading LGBTQ activists say, is that social perceptions, education, and some legal concepts and rules have not yet caught up with the scientific facts. Hence, transphobia remains ingrained in some quarters of society. As a result, ignorance-based dislike and fear of alternatively gendered people continue to motivate discrimination against them in public facilities, job hiring, military service, and other important social venues.

Bullying and Discrimination in Schools

Moreover, name-calling, bullying, and social exclusion aimed at trans and nonbinary students still exist in many schools. An example of such abuses in educational settings took place on Long Island, New York, in 2014. Mariah, who was born a biological male but from an early age identified as female, wore plastic sandals most often worn by girls on her first day in elementary school. The teacher gave her a disapproving look and said, "You're a boy. You're not supposed to go to school like this. Don't put on those [shoes] again!" Mariah defiantly continued to wear the sandals, however, and "one day," she recalls, "the teacher took me out of the classroom and pinched me hard," and said, "What's going on with you? You're a guy! Are your parents abusing you? Are you being raped? Are you being molested?"[52] Not only did the teacher say these totally inappropriate things to the five-year-old, she also reported the case to the local office of Child Protective Services, which investigated Mariah's family on suspicion of child abuse.

Mariah's case was not unusual. In elementary, middle, and high school, trans and nonbinary students suffer bullying and other forms of discrimination every day. A major 2020 national survey conducted by the noted LGBTQ education and advocacy group GLSEN showed that over 20 percent of alternatively gendered students are bullied each year. Furthermore, more than half of those questioned said they felt unsafe in school.

Such fears are well founded because some of the bullying escalates into physical violence. "I've been shoved into lockers," recalls Kevin, a trans high school student from Utah. Unfortunately for him, when he reported the abuse to the school administrators, they said it was his own fault. After all, they told him, instead of hiding his gender identification, as they felt he should have, he had been "so open about it."[53]

Bullying in schools causes more harm than the obvious physical and psychological damage. It also makes it much harder for the victims to learn, not to mention it turns some of them off to education in general. The scope of the problem can be seen in the results of GLSEN's 2020 study, which questioned students in all fifty states, the District of Columbia, and the US territories Puerto Rico, American Samoa, and Guam. One finding was that a disturbingly high 69 percent reported being verbally harassed in school. Meanwhile, a parallel study was conducted in 2020 by the *American Journal of Preventive Medicine*. It uncovered that an enormous proportion of American LGBTQ teenagers—91 percent—suffer bullying or discrimination at least once in their school careers.

A Twisted Blend of Racism and Transphobia

Discrimination and violence aimed at alternatively gendered people is not confined to the school years. Rather, these sorts of abuses often follow them into the adult world. Insulting remarks, threats, beatings, and worse against trans and nonbinary individuals occur in every state in the union each year.

Sadly, at times the most violent incidents end in someone's death. In June 2019, for instance, Chanel Scurlock, a twenty-three-year-old trans woman living in North Carolina, left her home to visit an acquaintance. A day later, her body was discovered in a field, and police reported that she had been fatally shot. In similar fashion, in March 2021 another trans woman, Diamond K. Sanders, also twenty-three, was shot to death in Cincinnati, Ohio. In that same month, Rayanna Pardo, twenty-six, of Los Angeles, died when a group of people harassed her and shoved her in front of a moving car. "Rayanna was such a beautiful young person who just wanted to live her life and be herself,"[54] one of her friends stated soon afterward.

Tragedies of this kind are not uncommon. The Human Rights Campaign, which keeps track of such incidents, says that forty-four trans people were murdered in the United States in 2020 alone. Furthermore, from 2013 to the end of 2020, more than two hundred transgender and nonbinary people were victims of anti-LGBTQ violence. According to the Human Rights Campaign, "These victims were killed by acquaintances, partners or strangers, some of whom have been arrested and charged, while others have yet to be identified. Some of these cases involve clear anti-transgender bias. In others, the victim's [gender] status may

46

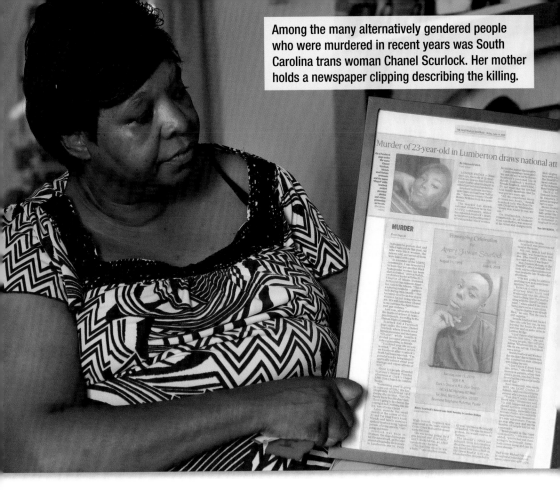

Among the many alternatively gendered people who were murdered in recent years was South Carolina trans woman Chanel Scurlock. Her mother holds a newspaper clipping describing the killing.

have put them at risk in other ways, such as forcing them into unemployment, poverty, [and] homelessness."[55]

Another troubling aspect of these crimes is that a disproportionate number of them target trans people of color, especially those who identify as female. Scurlock and Sanders were both Black women, and Pardo was Latina. In such cases, the victims were confronted with the twisted blend of racism and transphobia. These individuals "are marginalized, stigmatized and criminalized in our country," says Rodrigo Heng-Lehtinen, deputy executive director for the National Center for Transgender Equality. "They face violence every day." He adds that racism and transphobia "push so many transgender people of color into vulnerable situations, shut out of stable housing, secure jobs and loving homes. No one should be forced to live in fear."[56]

Legal Attempts to Discriminate

Even when they are not being assaulted or killed, alternatively gendered folk often face social and legal challenges that the vast majority of Americans do not. As Heng-Lehtinen points out, they are often cruelly disowned by their parents and blocked from getting good-paying jobs and decent housing. Moreover, all too often they face rules and laws purposely designed to discriminate against them.

Perhaps the most famous examples of such laws in recent years were the so-called bathroom bills passed mostly in 2015 and 2016 in Mississippi, North Carolina, and Texas. Some other states, along with several American cities, debated such bills, but only a few of them became law. The ones that did pass prohibited trans individuals from using public restrooms that match their gender identities. In other words, a trans woman could not enter a women's restroom, and a trans man was barred from entering a men's restroom. Those who created these statutes claimed they were afraid a man might put on women's clothes, enter a women's restroom, and attack an unsuspecting woman using the restroom. They also cited the possibility that a child molester might assault children in a public bathroom.

In contrast, opponents of the bathroom bills argue that such fears are groundless and even ludicrous. Noted legal commentator Ian Millhiser explains that no person "has ever been sexually assaulted by a trans woman in a bathroom." Nor, he states, has a man pretending to be a trans woman ever assaulted anyone in a bathroom. In fact, he says, the backers of such laws are never able to point to examples of such crimes. Millhiser adds that "the likelihood that a woman will face this kind of assault appears to be exactly the same as her chances of being attacked by a unicorn."[57]

> "[No person] has ever been sexually assaulted by a trans woman in a bathroom."[57]
>
> —Ian Millhiser, legal commentator

Such discriminatory laws sparked protests from trans and nontrans people alike, and a number of trans individuals chal-

Working to End Gender Discrimination

Liza Brusman, a graduate researcher in molecular biology at the University of Colorado, Boulder, is a strong advocate for treating alternatively gendered people with respect and kindness. To that end, she wants to see an end to various kinds of gender discrimination, and she suggests that legislation could be part of the answer. In an article she wrote for Massive Science, an online research site written by scientists for other scientists, she states in part:

> To truly put an end to sex and gender-based discrimination, we need legislation that considers sex as a spectrum with unlimited options. In some cases, this could be as simple as expanding the language that has been used in [some existing laws] to be explicitly inclusive of all sexes and genders. We also need laws that specifically protect people with non-binary sexes and genders from discrimination in areas like healthcare settings, the workplace, and housing. The science is clear—sex is a spectrum. Yet the solution to the misunderstanding of sex doesn't end with scientists. We also need better public education and structural changes to recognize and protect people and their biology.

Liza Brusman, "Sex Isn't Binary and We Should Stop Acting Like It Is," Massive Science, June 14, 2019. https://massivesci.com.

lenged those statutes in court. One of the several who won their cases was nineteen-year-old Drew Adams of Ponte Vedra, Florida. After the court ruled in his favor in August 2020, he stated, "High school is hard enough without having your school separate you from your peers and mark you as inferior. I hope this decision helps save other transgender students from having to go through that painful and humiliating experience."[58] The judges who rendered the verdict agreed that he had been treated as if he was somehow inferior to other students. In their unanimous support for Adams, those judges stated in part, "A public school may not punish its students for gender nonconformity. Neither may a public school harm transgender students by establishing arbitrary, separate rules for their restroom use."[59]

An Expanding Attack on Trans Youth

A number of other attempts to legally discriminate against alternatively gendered people have emerged in recent years and continue to appear. One that made headlines on and off consisted of attempts to prevent trans people from serving in the US military. President Barack Obama opposed such a ban, and in 2016 he lifted it. However, the following year President Donald Trump reinstated the anti-trans prohibition. Trans and other members of the LGBTQ community were relieved when President Joe Biden reversed Trump's ban in early 2021.

School sports has been another common social sphere in which alternatively gendered people have been targeted, say advocates for LGBTQ equal rights. One of several recent examples of state legislatures trying to bar trans and nonbinary athletes from playing surfaced in South Dakota in 2021. The bill's aim was to prevent trans female students from competing on teams matching

High school girls are seen here playing soccer. A legislative bill was proposed in South Dakota in 2021 that would have banned young trans women from competing on such teams.

their gender identity. Proponents of the new law argued that such students would have an unfair physical advantage against other girls because they are not actually girls. Like earlier attempts to pass such controversial bills, that one failed to pass. But some states continue to push for such legislation, and that worries some pro-trans advocates, including officials at the Human Right Campaign. One of its spokespersons stated in February 2021, "There is a coordinated attack on trans kids being waged in state legislatures across the country right now."[60]

> "There is a coordinated attack on trans kids being waged in state legislatures across the country right now."[60]
>
> —Human Rights Campaign

That attack seemed to expand in scope not long after those words were spoken. In April 2021 Republican lawmakers in North Carolina proposed a law that would prohibit doctors from performing gender-related surgery on trans individuals younger than twenty-one. The legislation would classify people age eighteen to twenty as minors. Even more extreme, according to pro-trans advocates, is a Texas law, also introduced in April 2021, that would label parents who try to help their transgender offspring as child abusers. Under this law, the children could be removed from the home and the parents jailed.

As for what can be done to counter such provocative and divisive measures, experts say that people everywhere should try to act humanely. They should accept that, whatever gender a person may identify with, a trans or nonbinary individual is a human being with the same feelings and needs as everyone else. Transphobia is unfounded, unnecessary, and cruel, the experts point out, and puts those who feel they are alternatively gendered at risk of physical and psychological harm. Understanding and compassion for those who are different than the norm should be the guiding principle, says Elliot Page, whose own experiences with alternative gender identity were exposed to public scrutiny. "If we could just celebrate all the wonderful complexities of people," he says, "the world would be such a better place."[61]

Source Notes

Introduction: Man into Woman

1. Quoted in Niels Hoyer, ed., *Man into Woman*, trans. H.J. Stenning. New York: Dutton, 1933, p. 31.
2. Quoted in Hoyer, *Man into Woman*, p. 113.
3. Quoted in Hoyer, *Man into Woman*, p. 64.
4. Quoted in Hoyer, *Man into Woman*, p. 31.
5. Quoted in Scarlett Conlon, "Eddie's Education." *Vogue*, August 12, 2015. www.vogue.co.uk.

Chapter One: Many Alternative Gender Identities

6. Quoted in Susan Kuklin, *Beyond Magenta: Transgender Teens Speak Out*. Somerville, MA: Candlewick, 2014, p. 4.
7. Quoted in Kuklin, *Beyond Magenta*, p. 8.
8. Quoted in Kuklin, *Beyond Magenta*, p. 25.
9. Alana Biggers, "What's the Difference Between Sex and Gender?," Healthline, 2019. www.healthline.com.
10. Karen L. Blair, "Has Gender Always Been Binary?," *Inclusive Insight* (blog), *Psychology Today*, September 16, 2018. www.psychologytoday.com.
11. Quoted in Katy Steinmetz, "Elliot Page Is Ready for This Moment," *Time*, March 16, 2021. https://time.com.
12. WebMD, "Non-Binary Sex: What It Is," 2020. www.webmd.com.
13. Archaeology News Network, "Grave of Stone Age Transsexual Excavated in Prague," April 6, 2011. https://archaeologynewsnetwork.blogspot.com.
14. Dio Cassius, *Roman History*, trans. Earnest Cary. Cambridge, MA: Harvard University Press, 1927, pp. 465, 471.
15. Quoted in Laurel Wamsley, "Rachel Levine Makes History as 1st Openly Trans Federal Official Confirmed by Senate," NPR, March 24, 2021. www.npr.org.
16. Quoted in Victoria A. Brownworth, "Dr. Rachel Levine: 'Stay Calm, Stay Home, Stay Well,'" Philadelphia Gay News, April 1, 2020. https://epgn.com.

Chapter Two: Being Transgender

17. Quoted in *New York Times*, "Hayden Reid," 2015. www.nytimes.com.
18. Quoted in *New York Times*, "Hayden Reid."
19. Quoted in *New York Times*, "Hayden Reid."
20. Quoted in Kuklin, *Beyond Magenta*, p. 8.
21. Quoted in *New York Times*, "Kimberly Moore," 2015. www.nytimes.com.
22. Jeffrey M. Jones, "LGBT Identification Rises to 5.6% in Latest U.S. Estimate," Gallup, 2021. https://news.gallup.com.
23. National Health Service, "Worried About Your Gender Identity? Advice for Teenagers," 2018. www.nhs.uk.
24. Quoted in Kuklin, *Beyond Magenta*, p. 5.
25. Quoted in *New York Times*, "Declan Nolan," 2015. www.nytimes.com.
26. Quoted in *New York Times*, "Cass Averill," 2015. www.nytimes.com.
27. Nicholas M. Teich, *Transgender 101: A Simple Guide to a Complex Issue*. New York: Columbia University Press, 2012, p. 119.
28. Quoted in *New York Times*, "Cass Averill."
29. Millicent Odunze, "Preparation and Procedures Involved in Gender Affirmation Surgeries," Verywell Health, December 13, 2020. www.verywellhealth.com.
30. Quoted in *New York Times*, "Loren Bornstein," 2015. www.nytimes.com.

Chapter Three: Being Nonbinary

31. Quoted in Kuklin, *Beyond Magenta*, p. 121.
32. Quoted in Kuklin, *Beyond Magenta*, p. 121.
33. Quoted in Kuklin, *Beyond Magenta*, p. 122.
34. Quoted in Kuklin, *Beyond Magenta*, p. 126.
35. GLAAD, "Transgender FAQ." www.glaad.org.
36. Kylan Camburn, "9 Young People Explain What Being Non-Binary Means to Them," GLAAD, July 14, 2019. www.glaad.org.
37. Quoted in Camburn, "9 Young People Explain What Being Non-Binary Means to Them."
38. Quoted in Kuklin, *Beyond Magenta*, p. 131.
39. Quoted in Rachel Hills, "4 People Explain What It's like Being Genderqueer," *Cosmopolitan*, April 28, 2017. www.cosmopolitan.com.
40. Quoted in Jackson W. Shultz, *Trans/Portraits: Voices from Transgender Communities*. Hanover, NH: Dartmouth College Press, 2015, pp. 72–73.

41. Quoted in Serena Sonoma, "Agender People Debunk Myths About Their Identities," INTO, January 14, 2019. www.intomore.com.

42. Quoted in Sarah Marsh, "The Gender-Fluid Generation: Young People on Being Male, Female or Non-Binary," *The Guardian* (Manchester, UK), March 23, 2016. www.theguardian.com.

43. Quoted in Yashee, "Cisgender, Agender, Bigender, Genderqueer: What Are These Terms, and Why Do They Matter?," *Indian Express* (Mumbai, India), September 3, 2020. https://indianexpress.com.

44. Meghan Werft and Erica Sánchez, "Male, Female, and Muxes: Places Where a Third Gender Is Accepted," Global Citizen, June 27, 2016. www.globalcitizen.org.

45. Quoted in Ola Synowiec, "The Third Gender of Southern Mexico," BBC, November 26, 2018. www.bbc.com.

46. Quoted in Synowiec, "The Third Gender of Southern Mexico."

47. Quoted in Sonoma, "Agender People Debunk Myths About Their Identities."

Chapter Four: Social Challenges of the Alternatively Gendered

48. Quoted in Adam P. Romero, "The Nineteenth Amendment and Gender Identity Discrimination," American Bar Association, May 6, 2020. www.americanbar.org.

49. Madeleine Roberts, "HRC Mourns Jeffrey 'JJ' Bright & Jasmine Cannady, Trans & Non-Binary Siblings Killed in Pennsylvania," Human Rights Campaign, February 24, 2021. www.hrc.org.

50. Gender Spectrum, "Understanding Gender." 2019. https://gender spectrum.org.

51. Quoted in Vincent Dowd, "Cured: How Mental Illness Was Used as a Tool Against LGBT Rights," BBC, March 25, 2021. www.bbc .com.

52. Quoted in Kuklin, *Beyond Magenta*, pp. 76–77.

53. Quoted in Human Rights Watch, "Like Walking Through a Hailstorm," December 7, 2019. www.hrw.org.

54. Quoted in Human Rights Campaign, "Fatal Violence Against the Transgender and Gender Non-Conforming Community in 2021," 2021. www.hrc.org.

55. Human Rights Campaign, "Fatal Violence Against the Transgender and Gender Non-Conforming Community in 2021."

56. Quoted in National Center for Transgender Equality, "Murders of Transgender People in 2020 Surpasses Total for Last Year in Just Seven Months," August 7, 2020. https://transequality.org.

57. Ian Millhiser, "How the Religious Right Learned to Use Bathrooms as a Weapon Against Justice," ThinkProgress, 2015. https://archive.thinkprogress.org.

58. Quoted in Lambda Legal, "Victory! Federal Court Rules Florida School Must Treat Transgender Students Equally Including Access to Restrooms," August 7, 2020. www.lambdalegal.org.

59. Quoted in Lambda Legal, "Victory!"

60. Ella Schneiberg, "These Are the States Trying to Stop Trans Kids from Playing Sports," Human Rights Campaign, 2021. www.hrc .org.

61. Quoted in Steinmetz, "Elliot Page Is Ready for This Moment."

Organizations and Websites

Family Equality Council
www.familyequality.org

The Family Equality Council supports and represents the 3 million parents who are gay, bi, trans, and queer in the United States and their 6 million children. The website offers information on how ordinary people, both straight and LGBTQ, can combat anti-LGBTQ discrimination in their communities.

Gender Spectrum
www.genderspectrum.org

Gender Spectrum works to make society more inclusive for alternatively gendered people. Its website allows visitors to join various pro-trans and nonbinary online groups for preteens, teens, parents, caregivers, and other family members.

GSA Network
https://gsanetwork.org

This organization's strategy is to fight for justice for LGBTQ people by empowering teens and others to educate the public on LGBTQ issues. The site offers a hands-on tutorial of how young LGBTQ people can build their own local support networks.

Human Rights Campaign (HRC)
www.hrc.org

The HRC deals regularly and frankly with gay, bi, and trans issues and problems. The website offers an array of links to articles that tell what is happening on the front lines of the LGBTQ struggle for equality, broken down on a convenient, easy-to-access, state-by-state basis.

National Center for Transgender Equality (NCTE)
http://transequality.org

The NCTE's mission is to help trans people enjoy equality and social justice, partly by educating politicians and other leaders about trans issues. The NCTE website contains helpful information about how trans and other LGBTQ people can lobby their congressional representatives.

Transgender FAQ, GLAAD

www.glaad.org/transgender/transfaq

The noted human rights organization GLAAD presents this well-written, informative general overview to transgenderism, explaining to teens and others the basic concepts, along with links to articles about related issues.

Transgender Law Center (TLC)

http://transgenderlawcenter.org

The TLC aims to alter public attitudes and laws that are harmful to trans and nonbinary people. Its website features two helpful programs— Positively Trans and Disability Project—that provide valuable legal information to alternatively gendered youth and their parents.

Transgender Legal Defense and Education Fund (TLDEF)

www.transgenderlegal.org

The TLDEF seeks to help end discrimination based on gender identity and to achieve equality for trans and nonbinary folk. The group's website provides links to recent online articles about trans-related legal cases, plus information about health care and education for trans individuals.

Trans Youth Equality Foundation (TYEF)

www.transyouthequality.org

The TYEF provides books, pamphlets, videos, and other educational materials, plus other types of support, for trans and nonbinary teens and their family members. Its website tells about trans-related workshops, camps, and podcasts and how to get involved in them.

TransYouth Family Allies (TYFA)

www.imatyfa.org

The TYFA supports and educates the families and friends of struggling trans and nonbinary individuals. Its website provides links to transgender-related educational programs, health care facilities, and a bureau that recommends guest speakers on trans and nonbinary issues.

Trevor Project

www.thetrevorproject.org

The Trevor Project is the leading national organization providing crisis intervention and suicide prevention services to LGBTQ people under age twenty-five. Its website contains contact information for individuals and groups that can help LGBTQ youth in crisis.

For Further Research

Books

Maria Cook, *Gender Identity: Beyond Pronouns and Bathrooms*. White River Junction, VT: Nomad, 2019.

Erin Ekins, *Queerly Autistic: The Ultimate Guide for LGBTQIA+ Teens on the Spectrum*. London: Jessica Kingsley, 2021.

Skylar Kergil, *Before I Had the Words: On Being a Transgender Young Adult*. New York: Skyhorse, 2021.

Eric Rosswood and Kathleen Archambeau, *We Make It Better: The LGBTQ Community and Their Positive Contributions to Society*. Miami, FL: Mango, 2019.

Robyn Ryle, *Throw like a Girl, Cheer like a Boy: The Evolution of Gender, Identity, and Race in Sports*. Ithaca, NY: Rowman and Littlefield, 2020.

Rebecca Stanborough, *She, He, They, Them: Understanding Gender Identity*. North Mankato, MN: Compass Point, 2020.

Jos Twist et al., eds., *Non-Binary Lives*. London: Jessica Kingsley, 2020.

Internet Sources

American Psychological Association, "Sexual Orientation and Homosexuality," 2021. www.apa.org.

Amnesty International, "LGBTI Rights," 2019. www.amnesty.org.

Elizabeth Boskey, "What Does It Mean to Be Genderqueer or Have a Nonbinary Gender?," Verywell Mind, November 30, 2020. www.verywellmind.com.

Kylan Camburn, "9 Young People Explain What Being Non-Binary Means to Them," GLAAD, July 14, 2019. www.glaad.org.

The Center, "What Is LGBTQ?," 2019. https://gaycenter.org.

Cornell University, "What Does the Scholarly Research Say About the Well-Being of Children with Gay or Lesbian Parents?," 2021. https://whatweknow.inequality.cornell.edu.

Vincent Dowd, "Cured: How Mental Illness Was Used as a Tool Against LGBT Rights," BBC, March 25, 2021. www.bbc.com.

Gender Spectrum, "The Language of Gender," 2019. https://genderspectrum.org.

GoodTherapy, "Gender Dysphoria," July 18, 2018. www.goodtherapy.org.

Rachel Hills, "4 People Explain What It's like Being Genderqueer," *Cosmopolitan*, April 28, 2017. www.cosmopolitan.com.

Human Rights Campaign, "Understanding the Transgender Community." www.hrc.org.

Lighthouse, "It's Science: Why Coming Out of the Closet Is Good for Your Health," 2021. http://blog.lighthouse.lgbt.

Kara Lowe, "Queer Students Navigate Dating Scene," Student Printz, November 15, 2019. www.studentprintz.com.

Alex Manley, "Your Guide to Gender-Fluid and Non-binary Relationships," AskMen, August 3, 2020. www.askmen.com.

Sarah McBride, "HRC Releases Annual Report on Epidemic of Anti-transgender Violence," Human Rights Campaign, November 18, 2019. www.hrc.org.

Frank Olito, "17 Celebrities Who Have Come Out as LGBTQ in 2020," Insider, December 28, 2020. www.insider.com.

Pew Research Center, "Chapter 3: The Coming Out Experience," June 13, 2013. www.pewsocialtrends.org.

Katy Steinmetz, "Elliot Page Is Ready for This Moment," *Time*, March 16, 2021. https://time.com.

Gabby Weiss, "10 Awesome LGBTQ Organizations to Support," Every-Action, May 20, 2020. www.everyaction.com.

Index

Picture Credits

About the Author

Classical historian and award-winning author Don Nardo has written numerous volumes about scientific and medical topics, including *Destined for Space* (winner of the Eugene M. Emme Award for best astronomical literature), *Tycho Brahe* (winner of the National Science Teaching Association's best book of the year), *The Science of Vaccines*, *Teens and Birth Control*, *Being LGBTQ*, and *The History of Science*. Nardo, who also composes and arranges orchestral music, lives with his wife, Christine, in Massachusetts.